One lazy gray afternoon, as I was humdrumming along, my imagination, apparently angry at being ignored, took a holiday—and never returned. I had lost what the poet Wordsworth called my "inward eye." Lost it, or simply left it lying about somewhere in the natural world.

What was I, an artist, to do? How was I to work, to paint, to live?

I tried clinging to scraps of memory, but they were never enough. Memories are old hat, my friend; imagination is new shoes. Having lost your new shoes, what else is there to do but go and find them?

The Last Resort

The Last Resort

Roberto Innocenti

J. Patrick Lewis

Creative Editions

Illustrations copyright © 2002 Roberto Innocenti

Text copyright © 2002 J. Patrick Lewis

Published in 2002 by Creative Editions

123 South Broad Street, Mankato, MN 56001 USA

Creative Editions is an imprint of The Creative Company

Designed by Rita Marshall, edited by Aaron Frisch

Printed in Italy

LIBRARY OF CONGRESS CATALOGING-IN-PUBLICATION DATA

Lewis, J. Patrick. The last resort / illustrated by

Roberto Innocenti; written by J. Patrick Lewis.

ISBN 1-56846-172-0

1. Artists—Fiction. 2. Artist's block—Fiction.

I. Innocenti, Roberto. II. Title.

PS3562.E9465 L37   2002   813'.54—dc21   2001047536

First Edition   9 8 7 6 5 4 3 2 1

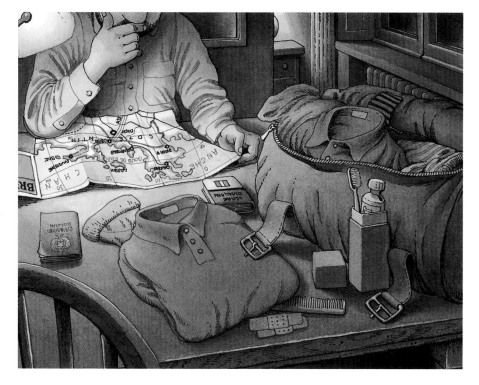

I put away my brushes and easels, packed my bag, and locked

up my little house. This was to be my green day of destiny.

Though I had no idea how or why, my red Renault seemed to

know the way. I was buzzing along a busy avenue to WHO-

KNOWSWHEREVILLE, when the car suddenly turned down a lane

as long as loneliness, past a cliff beyond forgetting, through a spider-lightning night.

At last the Renault sputtered to a stop at the foot of a most remarkable seaside hotel.

"Excuse me, lad," I said to the curious young man

at the door, "but where in the world am I?"

His face freckled up brightly from a book of prac-

tical magic, and he said,

 Evenin' stranger. Parrot's got you booked in

  Litrachoor,

 Where Answers dance with Question marks so

  you can find the cure.

 Your room's a-waitin' for you, sir. Leave every-

 thin' behind.

 This here's The Last Resort for folks who've

  lost a piece of mind.

"Well, thank you, my boy," I said, not knowing who he was or what he was going on about. He smiled, nodding toward the door. As soon as I opened it, a bird of a clerk squawked, "Please sign the guest register, pilgrim. Our maid will show you to your quarters."

I stared at the signatures in the guestbook. What were these chaps doing here? And what was *I* doing here?

My suite was blue-ribbon comfort. Having finished a King's meal in wonderment about the strangeness of it all,

I fell into bed with a full belly and a book, climbing over the ragged edge of dreams even before the sea had settled.

But just as I was dozing off, I remember hearing a loud knocking on the staircase. "Shiver my timbers!" the parrot screeched at me the next morning. "A funny fellow indeed," he explained. "He peglegs in here, signs the guestbook with crossbones—and climbs the stairs with his good leg and pegleg reversed. Now what do you make of that?

"By the way," the bird clerk chattered on, "our guests are all going after the odd bingdingle. What is so odd bingdingle about you, pilgrim?"

Odd bingdingle? Since my imagination had flown the coop, I admit I had become as dull as a glue pot, but still. . . . *Speak, Mistress Fanciful,* I thought, exasperated. *Say something!*

"All in good time, sir," the parrot winked, as if he had read my pennyworth thoughts.

Setting out for a walk, I found myself wishing that there really was something unusual about me, something unique. But what could it be?

Out on the pier, the lad I'd met the night before was fishing for . . . messages? His seasong was enchanting.

No other lands,

No other lives,

No other loves for me,

But the magical lands

And lives and loves

In the tales I fish from the sea.

What a lucky boy, I thought, to have found what he was looking for. But can imagination really be bottled like lemonade?

❧

That sprightly tune would not leave my head. Humming its refrain, I returned to the hotel, where I saw the fourth of the auberge's guests—a delicate,  sickly girl in white ruffles, accompanied by her nurse.

More bizarre still was a Mr. Gray Grayish. A black and white room suited his dullness perfectly. When the clerk bird asked him how he intended to spend his time, the little man replied, "By writing extraordinary letters." He was up to something, that much was certain, and he set to work immediately.

The fisherboy was absent at lunch, but the other five guests, including myself, welcomed silence,

each intently idle. What were we anticipating? The weather, the waters, the wonders ahead?

In the breezy hours after lunch, blues and whites quilted the sky. Sunlight fastened itself to the shore and would not let go. In her tented wicker sun-screen, the fragile young lady tired the sun with reading. Curiosity caught me up, and I stole a glance at the book she held, but could only make out *The Little Me—*. Her whispers, carried on the wind, reminded me of a story I'd heard as a boy.

I'm Mistress of the Ocean, I'm Bride of the Wave.

Someday I shall marry the land-man I save.

Some night he will fetch me in my seaside dress,

And Sea-witch, he'll hold me and all I possess.

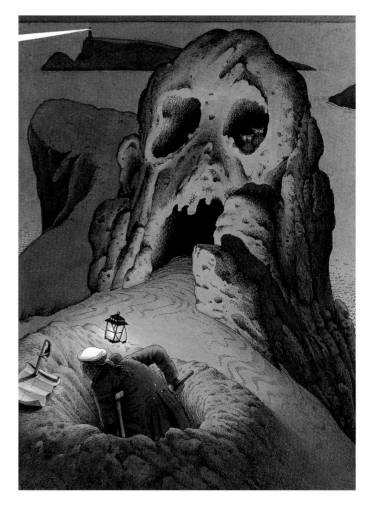

As the sun gave way to the moon, the night con-
tinued strange. The one-legged sailor, all lurch and
shamble, dug and dug with no luck at all.

I'll clap me eyes on the treasure, Jim Hawkins,

I'll find me a map that'll take me there.

I swear on a black-hearted pirate's dishonor,

Dooty is dooty. My share is your share.

Farther on, he tried another spot, digging in vain,
and all the while he was watched by a strange hom-
bre out of the wild west, seeking his own way in the
world, or so it appeared by the look of *his* scrolled map.

In the small hours before dawn, I heard the tall drifter shout after the sailor, "That map of yours is useless, Cap'n. I've got the real one. What I'm looking for, though, is a pale lady in white. She saved my life once. If you can tell me her whereabouts, my map is yours."

"You speak plucky enough, Rodeo. And by thunder I been a-diggin' half the night," said the seaman doubtfully. "But this here map o' mine is Bill Bones' own. I trust it'll trace to treasure before the tide rides full."

I must pay closer attention! I thought. If only I could unravel the purposes these strangers sought, I just might be able to recover the figments of my own imagination. But without it to rely on, I needed help putting the pieces together.

As if on cue, the police arrived unannounced at the inn. Perhaps the round Inspector could solve these odd cases. It seemed everyone here was searching for something. And something was hiding from everyone. Where would the tangled plots of these many mysteries lead?

The Inspector put it clearly in a vague sort of way:

All of the guests are under suspicion,

But under suspicion of what?

Ah, that is the singular aim of my mission:

Connecting the IF *with the* AND *or the* BUT.

Suddenly, the windows began to rattle! Outside,

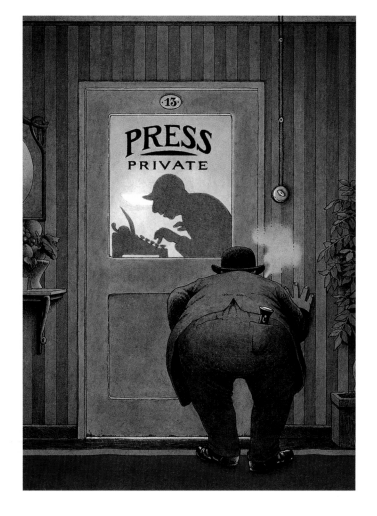

23

laughing gulls cried and puffins shuffled away at the roaring whine of a bi-plane overhead.

The sound tore at the sky as a wing broke, and the plane crashed into the sand!

Unharmed, the aviator nonchalantly crossed the dune. "Here comes another one just in for a flight of fancy," the clerk bird squawked, as if expecting him all along.

As that drama played itself out, the Inspector was deep in thought at the auberge's café. Irresistibly drawn to the aroma of roast chicken, he ventured out to the patio, where a peculiar Georgian gentleman was perched comfortably high in a tree!

Mon Dieu, thought the Inspector, *now I have seen everything!* "What mischief are you up to, spy-in-the-sky?" he asked.

Impatiently tapping his buckle shoe on a limb, the gentleman replied,

Don't mind me, sir, never mind me,

Sitting up here in my billyroot tree.

Life on the land, as a rule of thumb,

Becomes ho-hum and cumbersome.

Here, in the government of air,

There's far less fuss and much more care.

Here with the birds and the clouds, I might

Spy my hero, the windmill knight.

Windmill knight? Confused, the Inspector stood staring at him until the tobacco dried up in his pipe.

Just imagine the trouble I had interpreting all this strangeness! Inspector tailing sailor digging in vain,

nurse wheeling invalid girl out to end of pier, . . . and in! Her other companion, the moon, welcoming her to the

sea. *The Little Me*— book lover returning the favor by frolicking in the waves as effortlessly as a . . . *fish!?*

Ah, I need not weary you with all the dicey details of an eight-legged story you can picture for yourself. I turned blissfully to sleep, comforted by the hope that my nomad imagination stirred gently beneath my pillow. Such was the effect of this fascinating auberge, whose guests' intentions, I thought, a new dawn just might enable me to fathom—and to find what I was looking for in the bargain.

An Irish harp is my delight.

I went on dreaming half the night,

The other half I've yet to tell.

Sea chantey chanting casts its spell.

Meanwhile, the tall man of mystery stumbled upon his ocean jewel after all, and without the sea captain's help. The young lady in white was more important to him than any hidden treasure. At the same time, the ever-restless sea captain at last came upon the route to his own riches.

The next morning, life itself performed the greatest of sea sagas there on the beach! "Is that white whale waiting for high tide who I think it is?" I asked the aviator.

"*Mais oui*," he said, "who else could it be?

Foolish Captain Ahab has run aground chasing him."

Later, in the library, the clerk bird croaked, "Oi, my trusty Imaginers, new arrivals daily. Rooms must be vacated."

And so it was that some of the guests, their own quests ended, departed on a cobblestone road to fortune or folly, tomorrow or yesterday. Who could say?

Success had found the peg-legged sailor at last. Or he had found it with his new map, sailing off to El Dorado with the midnight tide. Was he searching for silver and gold? Spanish doubloons? Or something worth infinitely more?

One after another, the lodgers of The Last Resort seemed to find the fulfillment that still escaped me.

Morning had not yet broken when the aviator, too, set sail for new lands. Through means unknown to me, his broken bi-plane had been replaced by a well-built Lockheed P-38—the very model the fisherboy had assembled in the library the afternoon before. With a low drone, the plane wheeled away toward the still-sleeping sun.

As if in counterpoint to the majesty of that great flight, there on the inn's veranda, another spectacle was unfolding.

It is a rare occasion to see someone actually find his true colors. But that is exactly what happened to Mr. Gray Grayish.

Nonsense! Every word is gibberish! the Inspector grumbled to himself. *Gray Grayish must have used some secret code, except for that title—*An Autobiography Of Crimes! *Ah-ha! A* Capital Case. *I have found my man!*

Placed in handcuffs, the now colorful little man said, "I am not a criminal. I'm an actor by trade who, sadly, had lost his range of emotions. But I am

a wordsmith by nature. I play with words. The cryptic title An Autobiography Of Crimes came to me one night as I slept, and I've been searching for meaning in it until today. That title also says If I Am An Obscure Gray Photo. Same letters, different words: the perfect anagram.

"Don't you see, sir?" asked Gray Grayish. "I am not just an obscure gray photo. At least, not any longer. The Last Resort was my last resort, my inspiration."

How could the Inspector, ever the old softie, harbor doubt about a man with flowers on his hat? Besides, realizing now that the inn's guests were quite capable of solving their own cases, he could see that his services were not required. And so, by way of farewell, the policeman released the diminutive actor, but he couldn't resist offering him this tidbit of self-serving advice for his next film:

Bonne chance, adieu,

Sir Greenpinkblue.

I would play me

If I were you.

Afternoon burst into bloom when I spotted the latest arrival strolling along the beach. Pondering a couplet darkly, she whispered, as if speaking of The Last Resort itself:

We paused before a House that seemed

A Swelling of the Ground—

Oh, but I was delighted to hear her reciting. I have always believed that poems beg to be read aloud, even if the reader is in a world all her own.